PLEASE WASH
YOUR HANDS
BEFORE YOU READ ME
AND KEEP ME CLEAN

Today I am . . .

A Robot

by Jane Bottomley

IDEALS CHILDREN'S BOOKS

Nashville, Tennessee

It's time to decide what to be.

Let me look in the closet and see.

Today I am . . .

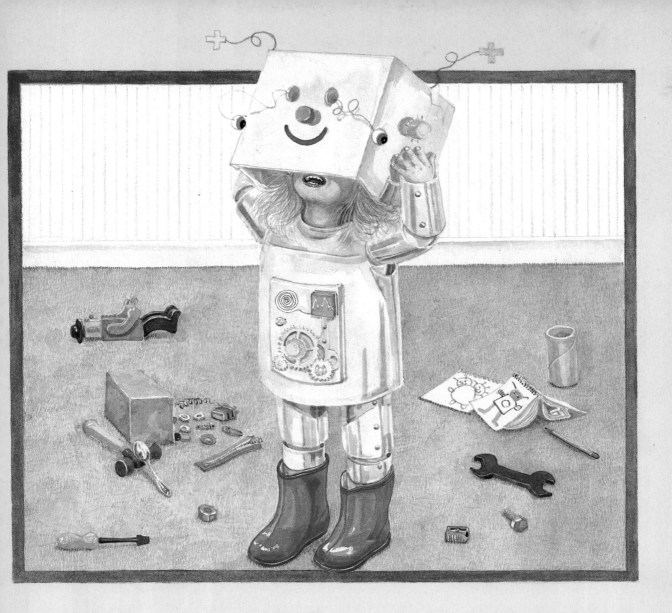

a robot!

I'm made out of metal and tin,

shiny bright and like a new pin.

I walk with a crash, a clink, rattle, bash –

how I like to make a great din!

In the park we play out in the sun.

I climb high and wave my ray gun.

Now we're off to the stars
to see planet Mars.

It's all such marvelous fun.

You can program what you want me to do.

I'm happy to tidy up too.

Just twiddle the dial,
and then with a smile

I'll carry your bag home for you.

When it's time to get ready for bed,
I need some help with my head.

Mom gives me a bath
and I splash and we laugh.

How nice to be ME instead!